PUT YOUR FUNNY SIDE UP!

In this book, Mike Thaler, America's Riddle King, shares with you his simple secret method of creating riddles. By following this method you will be able to create millions of funny riddles, and your own riddle books.

You will amuse your friends and amaze yourself!

Other Scholastic books by Mike Thaler, America's Riddle King:

The Moose Is Loose
The Square Bear and Other Riddle Rhymers
(with William Cole)

Funny Side Up!

How to Create Your Own Riddles

by Mike Thaler
America's Riddle King

SCHOLASTIC INC.
New York Toronto London Auckland Sydney

*To everyone in the world
who is a riddle kid at heart.*

Library of Congress Cataloging in Publication Data

Thaler, Mike
  Funny side up!

  "An Apple paperback."
  Summary: Shows how to write and illustrate riddles, using
famous names, rhymes, spelling tricks, common expressions, and
jokes.
    1. Riddles—Authorship—Juvenile literature.
  [1. Riddles—Authorship] I. Title.
  PN6367.T44   1985   808.06′87   85–2214

ISBN 0-590-33288-0

Copyright © 1985 by Mike Thaler. All rights reserved. Published by
Scholastic Inc.

12 11 10 9 8 7 6 5 4 3 2 1   7   5 6 7 8 9/8 0/9

TABLE OF CONTENTS

CREATING YOUR OWN RIDDLES

Hi, I'm Mike Thaler, America's Riddle King. I have created millions of riddles for my dozens of books. And the truth is — creating your own riddles is easy! In fact *it's easier to create riddles than to guess them*. And it's more fun, too! Through the years I have devised a simple four step method with which you now can create all the riddles you ever wanted to.

STEP 1
PICK A SUBJECT

Your subject can be anything in the universe. You can do cow riddles, cat riddles, bee riddles, bell riddles, star riddles, mouse riddles. You can make up riddles about school, sports cars or cooties. You can create riddles about *anything*! So let's pick a subject. How about pigs?

STEP 2
MAKE A LIST

Okay. We have a subject. **Pigs.** Now
we *make up a list of words* that mean
the same as **pig** or are closely associated
with **pigs**. This list is very important.
The more words on it, the more
riddles we can make. Okay, let's go.

Pig Words

Hog	Grunt
Boar	Oink
Swine	Pen
Sow	Mud
Swill	Ham
Slop	Sausage
Sueey	Hock
Snort	Pork
Snout	Piglet, etc.

The dictionary, the thesaurus, the encyclopedia, or any book on your subject will help you make this list.

STEP 3
PICK A FAMOUS PERSON, PLACE OR THING

Once your list is complete, *pick a famous person, place or thing*. Let's pick Albert Einstein. Okay, now divide his name into its syllables.

Al/bert Ein/stein.

There are four syllables. Now let's substitute a word from our pig list for one of the syllables. The pig word should *rhyme* with the syllable it is substituted for. The *closer* the rhyme, the *better* the riddle.

Okay, let's go. We can substitute *Swine* for Ein:

Al/bert *Swine*/stein

We can also substitute *boar* for *bert* which will make it:

Al/*boar Swine*/stein
or
Al/*boar* Ein/*swine*

Now pick the one you like the best. You now have your riddle answer.

STEP 4
MAKE UP THE RIDDLE QUESTION

Now that we have our answer, we have to *make up the riddle question*. Who was Albert Einstein? If you don't know, the encyclopedia, the dictionary, or any book on Albert Einstein will tell you. Now make up your riddle question from the most *important* facts about the person, place or thing.

Okay. ***What pig was a great twentieth century physicist, who thought up the theory of relativity?*** And the answer, or course, is:

Alboar Swinestein
        or
Alboar Einswine, whichever you like the best.

That's it. You've just made up your first riddle.

Let's review the four steps.

Step 1. Pick a subject.

Step 2. Make up a word list.

Step 3. Pick a famous person, place or thing. Divide it into its syllables, then substitute a word from your list for the syllable it rhymes with.

Step 4. Now make up your riddle question with the most important facts about that person, place or thing.

That's it!

Oh, wait a minute — there is a short cut.

SHORT CUT

Take any word on your word list. Let's take **ham**.

Drop the first letter, which makes it: **am**.

Now look in the dictionary, under words beginning with **am**.

We find: **America
ammunition
amnesia
ambush
ambulance**

Okay. *Make up your riddle questions*, then put your **H's** back on for the answers.

What great country has the most free pigs?
Hamerica.

What do you call a pig you shoot out of a cannon?
Hammunition.

What do you call it when a pig loses his memory?
Hamnesia.

What do you call it when a bunch of pigs jump out at you?
A hambush!

In what do you take a pig to the hospital?
In a hambulance.

Just to show it was no accident, let's take the word **pig**. We drop the **p** and get **ig**. Okay, look in the dictionary for words beginning with *ig.* We find:

> **igloo**
> **ignition**
> **ignorant**
> **iguana, etc.**

Okay, make up your riddle questions and put the **p's** back on for the answers.

What do you call an eskimo pig's house?
A pigloo.

How do you start a pig?
Turn on his pignition.

What do you call a pig that thinks making up riddles is hard?
Pignorant.

What do you get if you cross a pig with a lizard?
A piguana.

With some words you may have to drop more than one letter, as in **snout**. If you just dropped the **s**, you'd have **nout**. There are *nout* too many words like that in the dictionary. But if you drop both the **s** and the **n** you get **out**. And there are lots of words beginning with *out* in the dictionary:

> **Outfield**
> **Outfit**
> **Outlaw, etc.**

become:

> **Snoutfield**
> **Snoutfit**
> **Snoutlaw**

It is also a short cut to look at the words in the dictionary whose first syllables *rhyme* with your pig word.

Fig rhymes with **pig**, so **Fig Newton** would become **Pig Newton**.

What is a pig's favorite cookie?

A *rhyming dictionary* will help you in finding these words.

There are also many words whose first syllables may *almost* rhyme with your pig word.

Pic almost rhymes with **pig**, so **picture** can be **pigture.**

Picnic can be **Pig**nic.

Pick also almost rhymes with **pig**, so **pick**le can be **piggle**, and **pick**-up can be **pig**-up.

What kind of trucks do pigs drive?
Why pig-up trucks, of course.

You can also check the words that rhyme with the words that *almost rhyme* with **pig**.

Dic rhymes with **pic** so **dic**tionary could be **pig**tionary.

And it is also good to look in the *pig-tionary* for the words whose first syllable *is* your pig word. You may find some surprises like:

Pigment.
What do pigs paint with?

or

Pigmy or **Pygmy.**
What do you call a short pig?

Making up riddles is as easy as falling off a *hog*!

REMBRANDT VAN SWINE

When illustrating your riddles, just pick out the riddle's funniest aspect and draw it as silly as you can. *Be aware of the shapes of objects that look like pigs, or can be made to look like pigs.*

Be aware that many things, with a little help, can be made to look like other things.

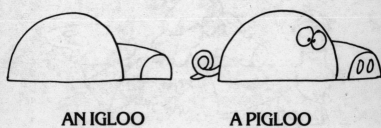

AN IGLOO   **A PIGLOO**

A WINE BOTTLE   **A SWINE BOTTLE**

AN OUTLET

A SNOUTLET

Okay. Got to it! Get a charge out of it!

A HAMBULANCE

A PIGNITION

HAMMUNITION

A SNOUTLAW

Have fun!

Oh, there's something else we should talk about. This isn't the only kind of riddle you can make up. *There are many different kinds of riddles.* Let me tell you about them.

KNOCK KNOCKS

First we have knock knocks.
Pick a pig word.
Pig
Now say it over and over and see what
word it sounds like.
Pig — Pig — Pick.
It sounds like **pick**.

Okay, *put it in a sentence.*
"**Pick** me up at eight-thirty."

*Change it back to pig and leave it in
the sentence.*
"**Pig** me up at eight-thirty."

That's your knock knock answer.

Now here's the knock knock question.
You say, *"Knock knock."* Your friend
says, *"Who's there?"*
You say, *"Pig."* Your friend asks, *"Pig
who?"* And you answer, **"Pig me up at
eight-thirty."**

Let's do another one.

Take **sausage**. Say it over and over and see what word or words it sounds like.

Sausage
Sausage
Saw Such.

It sounds like **saw such**.
Okay, put **saw such** in a sentence.
"I never **saw such** a smart person."
Now change it back to sausage.
"I never **sausage** a smart person."
That's your knock knock answer. Now do your knock knock.

"Knock knock."
"Who's there?"
"Sausage."
"Sausage who?"
"I never sausage a smart person."

HINK-PINKS, HINKY-PINKYS, AND HINKITY-PINKITYS

These riddles all have *two-word answers, and the two words in the answer have to rhyme.*

A **hink-pink** is two rhyming *one* syllable words.

A **hinky-pinky** *is two rhyming two* syllable words.

And a **hinkity-pinkity** *is two rhyming three* syllable words.

Okay, let's make up a *hink-pink*.
Take any one syllable word.
Pig.
Now find a word that rhymes with it.
Wig.
Okay, now put them together.
Pig Wig.

That's your riddle answer. Now make up your riddle question.

What do you call a pig's fake hair?
A pig wig.

Okay, let's do a **hinky-pinky**.

Take any two syllable word.
Piglet.

Now find a word that rhymes with it.
What about **wiglet?**.

Now put them together.
Piglet wiglet.

Now make up your riddle question.
What do you call a baby pig's fake hair?
A piglet wiglet.

28

Okay, let's make up a **hinkity-pinkity**.
Pick any three syllable word.
Piggily.

Now find a word that rhymes with it.
Wiggily.

Put them together.
Piggily wiggily.

or
Wiggily piggily.

Now make up your riddle question.
What do you call a sow belly dancer?
A wiggily piggily.

A rhyming dictionary will be very helpful to you.

Great! Now draw her.

A WIGGILY PIGGILY

ECHO RIDDLES

Now let's look at **echo riddles**. In an echo riddle the two words of the answer are *homonyms* or *homographs*.

What is a *homonym? A homonym is two words that sound the same but are spelled differently.*

Like: **see — sea.**

Okay, let's find some more homonyms:

> **Bare — bear**
> **Hare — hair**
> **Steel — steal**

These are all riddle answers. Let's make up riddle questions.

What do you call a hairless bruin?
A bare bear.

What do you call rabbit fur?
Hare hair.

What do you call a metal robbery?
A steel steal.

There are endless numbers of homonyms, so you can make up endless numbers of *homonym riddles.*

Okay, let's look at *homographs*. What is a homograph? *Homographs are two words that are spelled the same but mean different things.*

Like **sock — sock.**
One is something you put on your foot and the other is when you hit someone.

Or **punch — punch**.
One is something you drink and the other is when you hit someone.

Or **belt — belt.**

One is something that holds up your pants and the other is when you hit someone.

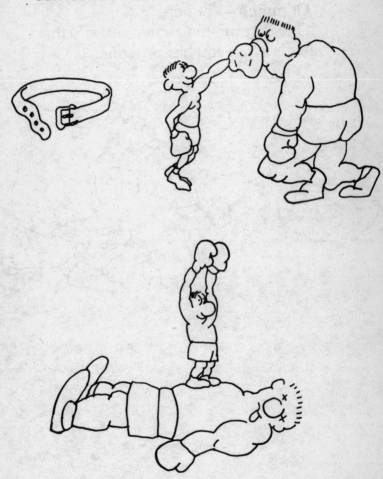

Let's find some *homographs*.

Pupils — pupils
Shrimp — shrimp
Husky — husky

Okay, these become our riddle answers.
Let's make up the riddle questions.

What do you call a student's eyes?
A pupil's pupils.

What do you call an extra tiny sea creature?
A shrimp shrimp.

What do you call an overweight sled dog?
A husky husky.

Now find some more *homographs* and make up some more *homograph riddles*.

CROSSES

Now let's look at **crosses**. Crosses are really regular riddle answers, put with this question.

What do you get if you cross a _____ *with a* _____ *?*

We already did one. Remember **Piguana**?
What do you get if you cross a pig with a lizard?

We can make cross riddles out of many of the riddles we have already done.

For instance:
What do you get if you cross a pig with Billy the Kid?
A snoutlaw.

What do you get if you cross a pig with an ice house?
A pigloo.

What do you get if you cross a pig with a bullet?
Hammunition.

You can make almost any riddle a cross riddle.

VISUAL RIDDLES

Now let's look at **visual riddles**, or as I call them, **"What is it?"** riddles.

In these riddles you give a picture first and ask, *"What is it?"*

For instance, this is my favorite visual riddle.

What is it?

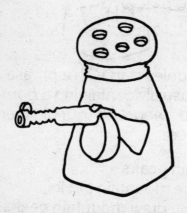

Assault with a deadly weapon
Which came from:
A salt with a deadly weapon.

I just realized something, if you change the drawing just a little . . .

It becomes — **a sultan with a deadly weapon.** *When you write and draw riddles be aware of words that sound like other words and objects that look like other objects.*

Visual riddles start with a phrase or sentence usually containing a *homonym* or a *homograph* (our old friends). For instance:

Mountain **peaks**
Could be mountain **peeks**,
Then you draw **mountain peeks**.

and ask, *What is it?*
Why, it's mountain peaks, of course.

Take the sentence **"A lady pursing her lips."** That could mean a lady putting her lips in a purse. Draw it,

and ask, *What is it?*

Of course, the answer is **"A lady pursing her lips."**

Visual riddles are endless. You have: **Railroad ties,**

A chain smoker,

A cop on the beet,

And a man having a light snack.

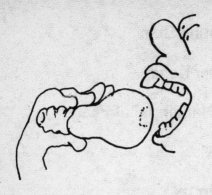

Draw them.
I particularly like
The Changing of the Guard

Here are some visual riddles for you to illustrate.

1. A Shooting Star.

2. A Rubber Band.

3. A Man Handing Out Fliers.

4. Foot Hills.

5. Shoe Horns.

6. A Man Stamping His Feet.

7. The Police Grilling A Suspect.

8. A Club Sandwich.

9. Fast Food.

10. A Boxing Match.

Visual riddles are lots of pun (I mean *fun*)!

PICTURE RIDDLES.

Picture riddles are also based on *homographs*, one word that means lots of things. Like **trunks**. There are many different kinds of **trunks** in the world.

Let's make a list.
>Swimming **trunks**
>Elephant **trunks**
>Traveling **trunks**
>Car **trunks**

Okay, *let's put them all in one picture.*

Now ask some friends to see how many **trunks** they can find in that picture.

There are many homographs that make perfect picture riddles, such as:

Decks
Bills
Bats
Bows

A dictionary, thesaurus, or grammar textbook may list other *homographs* that you can use for picture riddles.

MAGIC LETTER RIDDLES

Okay, let's look at **magic letter riddles**. In magic letter riddles, you change a word by taking away a letter.

   1. **Mice   ice**
  or two letters
   2. **Chair   air**
  or by adding a letter
   3. **Cat   scat**
  or two letters
   4. **Elf   shelf**

    Then, of course, you make up your question.

   By taking away what letter can you make mice cold?
   Take away their m and turn them into *ice.*

   By taking away what two letters can you make a chair disappear?
   Take away ch and turn it into *air.*

*By adding what letter can you
chase away a cat?*
Add *s* and make it *scat*.

*By adding what two letters can you
make an elf hold books?*
Add *sh* and turn an *elf* into a *shelf*.

Or you could ask it this way: *What
creature hides in a shelf?*
An elf, of course.

**What animal hides in a grape?
An ape.**

**What animal hides in a box?
Why, an ox is in there all the time.**

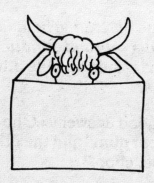

*See how many words you can find
hiding in other words.*

LIKE AND DIFFERENCE RIDDLES

Now we come to **like and difference riddles**. Here are some **like** riddles.

Why is a storm cloud like Santa Claus?
Because they both have rain, dear. (Reindeer.)

or

Why is a pig like ink?
They both run out of pens.

There's our old friend *homograph* again.
Here are some *difference riddles*.

What's the difference between a teacher and a railroad conductor?
One trains minds and the other minds trains.

Another good answer is: **One says "Spit out your gum" and the other says "Choo, choo, choo."**

So to make these up, find a pair of words that will take on a different meaning when the order of the words is reversed. One or both of the words will probably be a homonym.

More difference riddles:

trains   steers
steers   trains

What is the difference between a cowboy and an engineer?
One trains steers and the other steers trains.

or

bites   heels
heals   bites

What is the difference between a short dog and a doctor?
One bites heels and the other heals bites.

NONSENSE RIDDLES

Like and difference riddles bring us to **nonsense riddles** or **twist or trick riddles**. In these riddles, *the answers do not make any sense at all*. They are completely *silly!*

What do you get if you cross an ocean with a kangaroo?
Wet!

What do you get if you cross a cat with a vacuum cleaner?
I don't know but it sure drinks a lot of milk.

Or the classic:

What's red and green and purple with yellow spots and ten thousand legs?
The answer is, "I don't know, but it's crawling up your arm."

So you see, *you can make up riddles many ways, anytime, anyplace.* You can make them up *by yourself, with your mom or dad, with your teacher, or with any of your friends.* Then you can put them in a riddle book, make up a funny title and take it to your school library so that all the other kids can laugh at your riddles. If you ask the librarian nicely, maybe she'll put a regular pocket and a card in your book, and put your name in the card catalogue along with mine.

Then maybe she'll even put your book on a special shelf along with the books your friends have made and call it *Books by Us* or *Young Authors' Shelf*.

Maybe she'll even take a polaroid picture of you for the back of your book, and then you can write a little about yourself, *the author*.

You can honor someone special in your life by dedicating your book to them.

Then you can check out your own book and ask all your friends your riddles.

The riddle books you make are also *wonderful presents* for people you love.

Now, you can teach anyone who doesn't know how to make riddles just how easy it is.

So you see, riddles are *fun to make up, fun to ask your friends, fun to put in books* and *fun to see in your school library*.

Now you know everything I know about riddles and you can do everything I can do.

You are now all *Riddle Kings and Riddle Queens. So have fun!*

Learn a lot!

Laugh a lot!

About Mike Thaler

Mike Thaler, America's Riddle King, has created over eighty books for children, ranging from original riddle and joke books, to picture books, beginning readers, and fables. He is also the creator of "Letter Man" on TV's *The Electric Company*.

Mike tours America teaching kids how to create their own riddles and riddle books, and teaching teachers, librarians, and parents how to help them. He believes in *laughing with language* and *learning with laughter*.

**Riddle Books by Mike Thaler,
America's Riddle King**

The Moose Is Loose
**The Square Bear and Other Riddle
Rhymers*
Stuffed Feet
The Chocolate Marshmelephant Sundae
The Complete Cootie Book
Scared Silly
Never Tickle a Turtle
What's Up Duck?
*Give Up?
Paws
Oinkers Away
The Yellow Brick Toad
*Monster Knock Knocks
Mike Thaler's Riddle Rainbow:

Unicorns on the Cob
The Nose Knows
Grin and Bear It
Toucans on Two Cans
Steer Wars
Screamers
*Knock Knocks You Never Heard Before
*Knock Knocks The Most Ever
Funny Bones
Soup with Quackers

*with William Cole

If you want to send me a copy of your riddles, my address is:

Mike Thaler
America's Riddle King
Box 223, RD 1
Stone Ridge
New York 12484

Happy Riddling!

"RIDDLE KID"
OFFICIAL DIPLOMA

You are now an official Riddle Kid. You
are fully able to create your own funny
and original riddles, to illustrate them,
and to put them into riddle books.

Mike Thaler

Mike Thaler,
America's Riddle King